HELLO KITTY®

Goes to the Beach

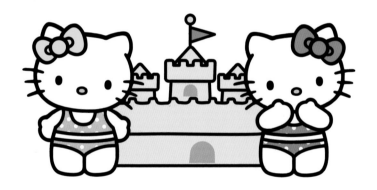

ABRADALE

New York

Today, Hello Kitty is going to the beach! She wakes up bright and early and looks out her window. The sun is shining and it's a perfect day for the beach.

Mimmy is already up and gathering things they'll need for the day. Time to get ready! Hello Kitty packs her sunglasses and her towel and puts on her bathing suit.

Mama packs a snack for everyone and reminds the girls to find their buckets and sand shovels.

Mama says that there are many fun things to do at the beach, like build a sand castle, go sailing, dig for shells, and swim!

At the beach, they find a nice spot near the water to spread out their towels. Tracy, Tippy, Thomas, and Joey are already there.

It is low tide, perfect for finding crabs and pretty shells. Hello Kitty likes to collect blue and green sea glass.

Time to build a sand castle! Don't forget the moat. A big wave splashes over them. Perfect, now there will be water for the moat. Should they make a drawbridge? This castle is going to have three big towers. A lovely princess will live there.

Next, it's time for a swim. Tracy wants to go surfing, and Hello Kitty dips her toes in the warm water.

Mama has a snack waiting for them on the
towels. Delicious homemade cookies! Everyone relaxes in the sand and soaks up the sun.

It's time to do some snorkeling now. Hello Kitty puts on her mask. What kind of fish will she see today? Maybe an octopus or even a whale? It's fun paddling around with the snorkeling mask on. Hello Kitty sees a pretty fish with orange stripes, and a horseshoe crab. They're so friendly!

Tracy offers to give Hello Kitty and Mimmy
a ride on his surfboard. He gives them each
a turn. The one who is waiting can jump
over the waves. There are so many great
things to do at the beach.

The waves are coming even farther up the shore now. Hello Kitty is worried the sand castle will sink! Mama assures her that the whole fun of sand castles is building them and watching them wash away, and then building more. You cannot keep castles made of sand.

Hello Kitty and Mama watch as the last tower disappears. They'll have to build another one when they come back to the beach the next time.

It is almost high tide now. Perfect for sailing.
Hello Kitty and Mimmy wave to Mama
and Tracy from the boat. Careful, the wind
is strong today. There is a rocky pier that
stretches far out into the water. Hello Kitty
steers around it.

Before it's time to go, Mama takes the girls
on a walk along the shoreline. They can each
pick one treasure to bring home with them.
Mimmy picks a beautiful starfish. Hello Kitty
picks a conch shell.

Mama says if you hold the conch shell to your ear, you can hear the ocean. Hello Kitty wonders if that's true.

Back at home, Hello Kitty and Mimmy think about all the fun things they did that day. They got to build a sand castle, go surfing, snorkel, walk on the beach, and go sailing.

Hello Kitty's favorite part of the day was
finding her conch shell. She puts it up
to her ear and hear the soothing sounds
of the ocean. Mama was right! Now she
can remember her day at the beach for
a long time to come.

ISBN 978-1-4197-0651-6

Printed and bound in China
10 9 8 7 6 5 4 3 2

THE ART OF BOOKS SINCE 1949
115 West 18th Street
New York, NY 10011
www.abramsbooks.com